the back of the book.

With special thanks to Conrad Mason

www.beastquest.co.uk

ORCHARD BOOKS

First published in Great Britain in 2018 by The Watts Publishing Group

1 3 5 7 9 10 8 6 4 2

A CIP catalogue record for this book is available from the British Library.

ISBN 978 1 40834 341 8

Printed in Great Britain

The paper and board used in this book are made from wood from responsible sources

Orchard Books
An imprint of Hachette Children's Group
Part of The Watts Publishing Group Limited
Carmelite House, 50 Victoria Embankment, London EC4Y 0DZ

An Hachette UK Company
www.hachette.co.uk
www.hachettechildrens.co.uk

NERSEPHA
THE CURSED SIREN

BY ADAM BLADE

BAY OF HEROES
JUNGLE

MAKAI

REDSTEEL FORGE

THE ELIXIR WELLS

CONTENTS

Quake before me, Avantians. You think you are safe in your distant kingdom, but you couldn't be more wrong.

All of Makai is under my control. This island's ancient Beasts are risen again and obey my every word. The people are my slaves, building a force unlike any you've ever seen. I will do what my mother, Kensa, and my father, Sanpao, never could...I will have vengeance on Tom and his people.

You can muster your soldiers. You can assemble your navy. But you will never be ready.

I'll be seeing you very soon.

Your soon-to-be ruler,

Ria

ARMADA

Tom gripped on tight to the gunwale, his gaze fixed on Ria. The pirate captain stood at the prow of the flying dinghy. The breeze ruffled her scarlet mohawk, and swayed the strands of the cat-o'-nine-tails which dangled from her right hand.

"It's over," she sneered, curling her lip. "You've failed."

Tom glanced over Ria's shoulder, feeling sick at the sight of the vast fleet of ships filling the distant bay. Some bobbed on the waves, moored just off the wide crescent of sandy beach. Others clustered in the skies above, swarming like vultures,

powered by the floating fuel Ria had mined from the Elixir Wells of Makai.

I was so sure I could stop her gathering a fleet, Tom thought. *But I was wrong.*

He gritted his teeth. Ria had

turned out to be an even deadlier foe than her parents, the witch Kensa and the pirate Sanpao. And if she were to bring her fleet to Avantia, there was no telling what destruction it would unleash.

Which is why I'm going to put an end to this, right now!

Drawing his sword, Tom leapt forward. But Ria was quicker. She swung her cat-o'-nine-tails and Tom ducked, feeling a sharp gust as the strands passed just above his head, crackling with blue electricity.

Ria laughed. "Do you understand how pointless your Quest has been?" she crowed. "What can one boy do against the greatest fleet ever assembled? My mother and father might have failed, but I will achieve what they never could...I'll raid your homeland, Tom. Oh, and I can't wait to reach Errinel! Your aunt and uncle will make such excellent slaves..."

Hot anger surged through Tom. He lunged, his sword flashing, but Ria easily sidestepped, and Tom's blade whistled through nothing but air.

With a grunt, Ria brought her flail round hard, smacking it on to Tom's shield. The impact sent him stumbling, his shin hitting the edge of the dinghy. He overbalanced.

"Goodbye, Tom," snarled Ria.

Panic rising, Tom swung his arms,

trying to recover. But Ria viciously lashed her cat-o'-nine-tails once again.

Szzzzzz! Tom's shoulder exploded with pain as the electrified strands

hit him. He clutched at the wound with his sword arm, but it was too late. He plummeted, dropping through the sky. As the treetops rushed towards him, he tried to lift his shield, hoping to use the magic of Arcta's feather to slow his fall – but his arm was dead, hanging limp and lifeless from Ria's blow.

He crashed through the uppermost leaves, then slammed into one branch that flipped him over as it cracked, then a second that knocked the wind from his stomach. Twigs lashed his face and snagged his clothes, before he struck the ground with a sickening *crack*. His ankle twisted, and he slumped to the earth.

He lay listening to his own heavy breathing. His body throbbed with pain in a thousand places. *But I'm alive...just!*

"Tom!"

At the familiar voice, Tom rolled cautiously on to his side, wincing with the movement. Elenna was running through the trees with Daltec, the wizard panting to keep up.

Elenna knelt at Tom's side. "Are you hurt?" she said.

Tom nodded. He unfastened the green jewel from his belt and held its cool surface against his ankle, drawing on its healing power. He felt a sharp burst of pain as a bone slid back into place. Then he flexed his foot. *Ouch! I'll be hobbling for a while...*

"Where's Ria?" asked Daltec.

Tom shook his head as he replaced the green jewel. "Sorry, she..." He grunted – it was an effort to speak. "She got away."

As Elenna helped him up into a sitting position, Tom saw more figures appearing through the trees. He recognised some of them – they were the villagers that Ria had enslaved to cut timber for her ships. Many of them still had iron cuffs and chains trailing from their wrists and ankles, but Tom saw one older villager going among them with a key, releasing them one by one.

A young boy with a mop of black hair rushed up to Tom, a slingshot poking out from his belt. It was Isaac, the boy whose life Tom had

saved in his battle with Jurog. Isaac stared at Tom's wounded shoulder with wide eyes. Tom realised that his tunic was ripped and the skin scorched black by the flail. "Did Ria do that?" asked Isaac.

Tom nodded. "I'm sorry I couldn't stop her."

"You saved us all, Tom of Avantia," said a man with matching black hair, laying a hand on Isaac's shoulder. "You have nothing to apologise for."

Tom did his best to smile, but he couldn't help remembering what he had seen from high up above the forest...

"Ria's fleet is almost ready," he told Elenna and Daltec. He could feel his strength returning now, along with his determination to finish the Quest. "I saw it anchored in a huge bay on the coast. It can't be long before Ria sets sail for Avantia."

"Then we must stop her," said Elenna, narrowing her eyes.

"And we'll help," said the man with black hair. "I'm Isaac's father, Ezra. We owe you our freedom, Tom. We'll fight alongside you."

Tom shook his head. "You're brave people, but I can't allow that," he said. "It's too dangerous. You can't take on a whole army of pirates."

"Perhaps I can help," said a female voice nearby.

Turning his head, Tom saw a slim,

red-haired woman, perhaps fifty years old, rubbing at her wrists where the manacles had just come off. "My name is Mathilde," said the woman. "I used to work at a water mill near the coast, and I know the

rivers here better than anyone. The bay where Ria is amassing her fleet is called the Bay of Heroes. There's a stream that leads to a cove right next to it, out of sight. If we could get there, perhaps you could find a way to defeat the armada."

"It's worth a try," said Elenna.

"Agreed," said Daltec. "But once we get there, we'll still be facing an entire fleet! How will we ever defeat such an impossible foe?"

"I don't know yet," said Tom. "But we'll find a way. While there's blood in my veins, that invasion force will never reach Avantia!"

1

THE FOUR MASTERS

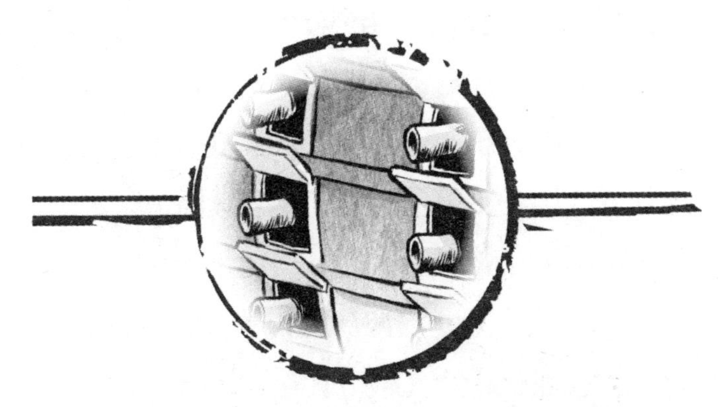

"Finished!" said Elenna, tying off the final rope.

Tom stepped back to admire the raft that rested on the muddy slopes of the riverbank. He, Elenna, Daltec and a crowd of villagers had built it out of timbers cut for Ria's fleet. Mathilde had even fixed a plank of wood to the back, making a simple rudder to steer them through the water.

"It'll do nicely," said Tom. "Now, when I say heave... Heave!"

All the villagers took hold of the raft and pushed, sliding it down the bank and into the shallows. Tom could feel the current tugging at it, as though the river itself was anxious to carry them off on their Quest. He rubbed at his shoulder – the wound would need dressing at some point, but it didn't sting nearly as much now.

Elenna held the raft as Tom turned to young Isaac. "Goodbye," he said, and the boy threw his arms round Tom's neck in farewell.

"Stay safe," said Ezra, shaking Tom's hand.

Mathilde stepped lightly on to the raft and sat cross-legged at the stern, taking hold of the tiller. "We'd better hurry," she said. "Ria will be anxious to set sail from the Bay of Heroes."

Tom clambered on board, followed by Daltec. Last came Elenna, and she gave them a shove off from the bank.

At once, the river carried them downstream as Tom and Elenna waved to the villagers. Then they curved round a bend and they were alone, with nothing but the trees of the forest looming all around.

Mathilde steered with skill, avoiding the bigger rocks and

branches that occasionally stuck up from the surface. Soon the river forked, then forked again, splitting into narrow tributaries that ran through the forest. Their navigator

always seemed to know exactly which path to take.

Tom stayed silent, thinking about the fight ahead. The pain in his shoulder had faded, and he felt ready to face Ria once again.

"Why did you call it the Bay of Heroes, Mathilde?" asked Elenna.

"You've never heard the story?" said Mathilde. "They say it was from there that the four Masters of the Beasts set sail, after they had defeated the wicked Eris and her four Beasts." She sighed. "I never dreamed those terrifying creatures would return. Or that another Master of the Beasts would come from a foreign land to face them."

She smiled at Tom. "All the islanders of Makai owe you thanks, Tom."

Tom shook his head. "There's no need. I'd do anything to help those who can't defend themselves."

Mathilde nodded. "We've lived in fear of the pirates for centuries, and it's about time someone stood up to them." Her face fell, and tears sprang into her eyes. "My sons...Ria took all three of them. She forced them to become sailors in her fleet. They're at the Bay of Heroes now, and when Ria invades Avantia, she'll take them with her." She dashed her tears away. "If I could get my hands on Ria...but no one could defeat her alone. What we need is a leader – someone to unite the islanders she has enslaved, and turn them against her." Tom felt her sharp gaze fall on him.

"I'll do what I can," he promised.

"Look!" cried Daltec from the prow, pointing to the sky.

Peering up, Tom saw dark shapes hovering like hornets, high above the treetops. *Ria's fleet!* The vessels were floating in midair, powered by the same Floating Elixir that had once carried Sanpao's ship aloft. Tom knew that every one of them would be crammed full of pirates, with weapons forged out of the redsteel that Ria had dug out from Makai's mines. *She's taken everything from these people!*

The raft ran quicker as the stream

wound its way downhill, carrying Tom and his friends through a rocky valley where the trees gave way to sky. Then they passed through the shadow of a deep ravine, so narrow he could almost touch the sides.

At last they emerged, bobbing, into a small cove with steep cliffs rising all around. *It's just as hidden as Mathilde promised...*

Tom caught his breath. Out in the bay, he could see the edge of Ria's water-borne fleet, huge galleons riding the waves. No doubt they would take off too, once the elixir was loaded on board. Every ship flew the same flag from her masthead. It was purple, with a

Beast skull emblazoned on it, just like Captain Sanpao's old flag. But this skull had whip-like tentacles streaming out, like the strands of

Ria's cat-o'-nine-tails.

Crunch! The raft juddered to a halt and threw them all off balance. Mathilde had run it on to a pebbled beach.

"Follow me," said Tom, drawing his sword.

His heart pounded as he led the way across the beach to a rough pathway gouged into the cliffside. It climbed steeply upwards, and Tom scrambled as fast as he could, his friends panting as they came behind. His shoulder stung with every step, spurring him on. *I'm coming for you, Ria!*

It wasn't long before they came out on the clifftop, where a stiff breeze cut through Tom's tunic and swayed the long grasses that grew in clumps among the rocks. Tom drew on the power of the golden helmet, part of the magical suit of armour that stood in the king's palace back in Avantia. His eyesight improved a hundredfold as the magic flowed through him. He peered out over the Bay of Heroes. He could see pirates on the beach, overseeing as villagers loaded barrels, cannon and shot on to longboats, some of which were already making their way out to the galleons in the bay.

The sight of the fleet took Tom's breath away all over again. It was even bigger than he'd imagined, ships cluttering the water as far as he could see. Some of the longboats were rising up into the sky like wasps, powered by Floating Elixir as they carried bundles of redsteel weapons and sacks of gunpowder to the fleet that drifted in the skies above.

"We can't let her reach Avantia," murmured Elenna, at Tom's side. "Can you imagine the damage she could do with this armada?"

Tom thought of the defenceless fishing villages on the Avantian coast, and of how the pirates would swarm ashore and maraud across the land, looting every settlement they came across, burning down houses, before they came at last to King Hugo's castle…

He shook his head, trying to clear the images from his mind. Mathilde and Daltec had arrived too, both dumbstruck by the size of the fleet.

Then a ship caught Tom's eye – a vast galleon, twice the size of Sanpao's old vessel, the sides gleaming with rows of cannons. It was hovering in midair, in between the two fleets, and a long anchor chain stretched down to the waves below. The sails were all purple, and each one carried the giant emblem of the Beast skull with trailing tentacles.

That must be Ria's flagship!

Through the magic of the golden helmet, he could see the figures on

the deck, scurrying to stow barrels in place. Ria moved among them, barking out orders, flailing with her lash when the sailors moved too slowly for her liking.

"I see her!" said Tom. *But how am I going to reach her...and even if I do, how can I stop such a massive fleet?*

A WATERY GRAVE

"It's hopeless," said Daltec. The wizard had gone very pale. "What can we do against such a mighty force of ships?"

"They might not be all that mighty," said Elenna, thoughtfully. "Tom, do you remember how we blew up the floating rocks of the Elixir Wells? If we could somehow set light to the gunpowder stores on board, we could destroy each ship, one by one."

"Good idea!" said Tom. "We'd need to get word to the conscripts somehow..."

"My boys can help," said Mathilde. "If we can just get the message to them, they could pass it on to the other conscripts. It won't take much to turn them against their captors."

"I'll go," said Elenna, quickly. "How do I get to the beach?"

Mathilde pointed to another path that led down the opposite cliff face. "My sons will be easy to spot," she said. "They have the same red hair as me. Take my shawl too, in case the pirates recognise you."

Elenna nodded, wound the shawl round her head then sped off to the path. In moments she had disappeared, scrambling down towards the beach.

"What about Ria?" said Daltec.

"Leave her to me," said Tom, hefting his sword. "Daltec, can you create a distraction? Something that will let me sneak past all those ships..."

The wizard frowned, deep in thought. Then a smile spread across his face. "I think I have just the thing."

Turning back to the hidden cove, Daltec raised his hands, pointing

them at the pebbled beach. A pale blue light glimmered around his fingertips, then – *Ffffzzzz!* – three blue sparks shot through the air, darting towards the raft. The blue lights flashed suddenly white, so bright that Tom had to blink. When he looked again, he saw that there were three figures sitting on board the raft – Daltec, Elenna...and Tom himself.

"Just an illusion, of course," said Daltec. Tom saw that his hands were trembling, and sweat had broken out on his brow. *It must be exhausting to maintain such a spell...*

"It's perfect," said Tom. "Thank you, Daltec!"

"I'll have to stay here, within sight of the illusion," said Daltec.

He flicked his hands, and the raft moved off, drifting over the water towards the entrance of the cove.

"Mathilde, you stay with him," said Tom, and the red-haired woman nodded. Then he raced back down the cliffside path, crossed the beach and waded out into the sea.

The water soaked Tom's trousers and clamped icily on to his skin. He took a deep breath, then dived in, swimming to the raft. He grabbed hold of it and pushed, kicking with his legs. Up close he could see that the figures on the raft were blurred and slightly see-through. *But they should be enough to grab the pirates' attention!*

Tom rounded the rocks, pushing the raft into the Bay of Heroes. He kept his head down low, so that he wouldn't be seen as he guided the raft on towards the fleet. When he caught sight of Ria's massive flagship, he sucked in a lungful of air and ducked under, steering the raft towards the vessel.

Opening his eyes, Tom saw anchor chains falling all around him through the turquoise depths, a maze of them covered in rust and barnacles. Shoals of fish swam here and there among the chains, darting away when they came too close to the dark hulls.

A sudden sound came through

the depths, a strange, eerie call like whale song. Something about it sent a chill down Tom's spine. *That's not a whale...*

Tom felt a surge of water as something passed beneath him. He glanced down and saw a shadow flitting in the depths, too fast to make out. Something big, almost as large as the ships which hung in the water above him.

He kicked harder, heart racing.

BOOM!

Tom flinched at the sound. It came from up ahead, muffled by the water. It was answered by similar sounds, ringing out all across the bay.

Cannons!

Tom heard a splash nearby, then another, and he saw cannonballs arcing through the water, sinking fast.

They're aiming for the raft! Daltec's distraction is working...for now.

Tom could feel his chest tightening, and he knew that he would need air soon. But the anchor chain of Ria's flagship loomed ahead, thick as a tree trunk, getting closer with every kick. Tom let go of the raft at last and powered beneath it, reaching out for the massive links of the chain. His hands closed around one, and he saw that it had the fiery sheen of redsteel. He began to haul himself upwards, climbing hand over hand. Breaking through the surface, he gulped in air and blinked as the sea salt stung his eyes. His feet found the links of the chain and he scrambled on upwards, as fast as he could.

If any of the pirates see me, I'm finished!

BOOM! The whole chain shook as one of the cannons on Ria's flagship fired. Tom clung on tight, his knuckles white with the effort. His ears rang. Up above the water, the gunfire seemed a hundred times louder. He cast a glance back at the raft, and the ghostly figures kneeling on it. The water all around it was choppy from the impact of cannonballs, but the figures stayed motionless. *How long can we fool the pirates?* Further away, on the clifftop, Tom could just see two specks – Daltec and Mathilde, watching the raft from afar.

Keep the illusion going, Daltec, thought Tom. *I'm counting on you...*

"Faster, you swabs!" roared a familiar voice from above. "Reload, at the double!"

Tom peered upwards and his heart stopped as he saw Ria leaning out over the gunwale, scowling at the raft. He froze, hoping desperately that she wouldn't spot him.

"Ready!" yelled Ria. "Aim... Fire!"

BOOM!

Another cannon near Tom jolted backwards, belching smoke. He craned his neck to see a spray of splinters burst from the raft. When the smoke cleared, the vessel was nothing but wreckage, floating on the waves.

Ria threw back her head and punched the air. "Victory!" she howled. "Farewell, Master of the Beasts. Enjoy your cold, watery grave!" She slammed her fist down on the gunwale then turned, striding across the deck.

Seizing his chance, Tom shinned up the last length of anchor chain and vaulted lightly on to the deck of the flying ship. He drew his sword, heart pounding as he took in the scene. The deck was crammed with pirates and conscripted islanders, but they were so busy with the cannons that they didn't notice him.

Tom spotted Ria, still facing away from him as she prowled the deck. He darted towards her, lifting his sword up high...

BEAST FROM BELOW

Tom's boots thundered on the deck. Ria whirled round, her eyes widening in shock. Then, with lightning speed, she swung her cat-o'-nine-tails. At the same instant, Tom swiped with his sword, and there was a crackle of electricity as the strands of Ria's weapon tangled around the blade.

Ria pulled him closer, brow creased

with confusion. Then she smiled. "The raft was a cheap magic trick, I assume?" she said. "Never mind, I've got you now.'

But Tom shoved into her with his shield, throwing her off balance as he tugged his sword free. Glancing round, he saw pirates closing in on all sides, their weapons gleaming as they rushed towards him. *I can't let them surround me!*

He rolled backwards, springing up again with his back to the gunwale. Still the pirates came on, grinning with savage glee. Beyond them, Tom saw a few terrified faces – conscripts, no doubt, who wanted no part in Ria's plans.

"You just won't give up, will you?" said Ria, pushing her way through the crowd of pirates. She was grinning too, twirling her cat-o'-nine-tails in circles, the weapon making a faint humming sound. "Where is that bumbling oaf you call a wizard? He must be here somewhere – along with that runt Elenna..."

I wonder how Elenna's doing looking for Mathilde's sons...

Tom tried to catch the eyes of the conscripted sailors. "Listen to me!" he called. "We can defeat Ria and her pirates, but only if we work together. Do you understand?" But none of the sailors would look at him.

Ria hooted with laughter. "You think these worms can save you, Tom? Look at them! Cowards, to a man! They're far too frightened of me...and of my little pet."

Tom frowned. *What pet?*

"Oh yes," said Ria. "You didn't know about her, did you?"

A distant screech rent the air.

Tom felt a prickle down his neck, and his blood ran cold. He knew that sound: it was the same eerie call he had heard underwater – but it seemed louder now, and more ferocious.

Tom turned, just in time to see a fountain of spray as something huge breached the surface of the water, near the cliff where Daltec and Mathilde stood. The sailors let out gasps of horror and disbelief, crowding closer together. Tom caught his breath.

It was a Beast, gigantic in size, with the body of a woman and the tail of a fish. Her skin was covered in black scales that shimmered like oil, and her hair was a ragged mass of green, like writhing seaweed.

The Beast arched her body, flicking away seawater in midair. She thrust out a hand, burying it into the cliffside. A shower of rocks went tumbling into the ocean, and Tom saw then that it wasn't a hand at all.

It was a dagger with three blades instead of fingers, each forged of redsteel.

Heart racing, Tom watched the Beast begin to claw her way up the cliff-side, her finned tail wriggling horribly, red eyes glaring upwards. Tom saw Daltec and Mathilde backing away from the cliff edge, and could only imagine the fear that must be gripping them.

"Ah – there's the wizard!" said Ria, cheerfully. "I knew Nersepha would sniff him out. She will be your doom!"

"Mother...?" murmured someone close by.

Tom looked around and saw a

skinny young sailor with a shock of red hair, his face white as he gazed at the cliff. *He must be one of Mathilde's sons, with that red hair!*

"I'll defeat Nersepha," Tom called to him. "I promise!"

Ria laughed. "Will you, indeed?"

Nersepha had almost heaved herself all the way to the top. She pulled her dagger hand from the rocks, dislodging boulders that bounced into the sea. Then, with the force of a battering ram, she drove it in again, right beneath the ground where Daltec and Mathilde were standing. A distant rumbling reached Tom's ears.

"Get away from there!" shouted

Tom. But it was no use. The clifftop crumbled away, collapsing like a heap of sand. Daltec and Mathilde fell with it, tumbling helplessly. Tom saw Daltec catch hold of a jutting rock and cling on, with his feet dangling in

the air. *He's so tired from conjuring that illusion, he can't use magic to save himself...* But Mathilde kept falling. Tom could do nothing as the brave woman went plunging down the cliff-face, faster and faster until – *SPLASH!* – she disappeared into the waves below.

"No!" the boy screamed. He lunged forward, but a tattooed pirate caught him and held him back.

"Well, I'd love to stay and watch the show," said Ria. "But we have a kingdom to conquer! Your kingdom, Tom, to be precise."

The pirate captain unhooked a horn from her belt, raised it to her lips and blew. The note rang out, loud and clear across the bay. "Set sail!" called Ria, and pirates across the galleon took up the cry.

Tom looked up and saw the airborne armada unfurling sails, moving off like a swarm of insects. He looked down and saw the fleet below moving too, anchors being weighed, sails filling with wind.

The invasion is beginning!

Tom cast a glance at Ria, still smirking among the pirates who crowded in all around. *I need to defeat her and stop this madness... But if I do that, who will save Mathilde?*

DANGER
DESTINY
1

THE CALL OF NERSEPHA

With a sick feeling, Tom made a decision. "This isn't over, Ria," he promised. Then he spun, put one boot on the gunwale and launched himself off the edge of the ship.

"Stop him!" screeched Ria, but it was too late. Leaping through the air, Tom aimed for the anchor chain. His arms closed round it and he clung on tight, muscles burning as he held on in midair. Then he felt himself hoisted higher, as the pirates began to wind up the chain...

No time to lose. Tom sheathed his sword, reached around the chain and took the handles of his shield, one in each hand. Then he let go with his legs, so he was dangling from the shield. At once it began to slide down the links of the chain, bumping and jolting as it went.

It was all Tom could do to hang on as the shield sped up, gliding downwards faster and faster. The wind buffeted him, and his teeth rattled in his skull as he juddered

towards the sea.

At the last moment he let go with one hand.

SPLASH!

He plunged into the waves, and all sound was muffled.

Tom kicked out, surfacing and drawing in a deep breath. Slinging his shield on his back, he swam as fast as he could towards the cliff where Mathilde had fallen. He could just make her out in the distance, floundering in a crash of white spray. The waves were buffeting her, pushing her closer to the jagged rocks at the foot of the cliff.

Nersepha's eerie call rang out once again, making Tom's blood run cold. It seemed to come from every direction at once, as though echoing from the rocks around the bay.

Tom kicked harder. He was nearly there now, close enough to see Mathilde's terrified expression.

"Tom!" she shouted. "Help me, please! That Beast is going to—"

The words were snatched from her mouth as the ocean erupted, a gigantic black hand closing around Mathilde's waist. Nersepha surged up from the water, casting a shadow over Tom, droplets cascading from her slick, glistening scales. Mathilde jerked helplessly in her grip, like a mouse under a cat's paw.

Welcome, Master of the Beasts...

The cold, hissing voice filled Tom's head out of nowhere. But he knew that it was Nersepha, speaking through the magic of the red jewel in his belt. The grotesque mermaid-Beast glowered down at him, her red eyes like fire underwater.

"Let her go!" said Tom, treading water as he drew his sword.

Oh, I think not, Tom. Nersepha leant down closer, her seaweed-hair falling over her face. She bared her teeth – each one as jagged and deadly as a shark's. *Do you know how long I have waited for my revenge? After I have feasted on this morsel, I shall feed on the Avantian dead... Every one of them, Tom, once Ria has laid waste to your homeland. Never again shall a Master of the Beasts defeat me!*

Nersepha let out a strange, harsh bark, like a seal's cry, and Tom realised with a shudder that she was laughing. He gripped his sword hilt tighter.

And do not think I shall stop there, Tom! The kingdom of Rion will be next. Then Gwildor. Then Tangala... I shall feast on them all!

Nersepha laughed again, and Tom wrinkled his nose as a gust of fishy breath washed across him.

Thud! The Beast jerked back, and Tom saw that an arrow had lodged in her shoulder. Nersepha shook her hair furiously. *Who dares attack me?* she raged. Then her eyes fixed on a figure, standing on the distant beach.

Tom followed her gaze. *Elenna!* His friend was already fitting another arrow to her bowstring. Pirates ran towards her, but with a leap of his heart, Tom saw a gaggle of conscripted sailors rush to Elenna's side, forming a ring around her and fending off the pirates

with spears and pikes. The tallest had bright orange hair – just like Mathilde.

Whhhsh! Elenna let fly with another arrow, then another, and Nersepha had to swipe the deadly

missiles aside with her dagger hand. The Beast was still clutching Mathilde in her other fist.

This is my chance! Tom realised. Summoning the power of the Golden Armour, he felt magical energy flow into his arms and legs. Then he struck out again, swimming straight for Nersepha.

Tom swung his sword as hard as he could, but Nersepha saw him coming. She met the blow with one prong of her dagger hand. *CLANG!* Tom's whole arm shuddered with the impact.

Nersepha drew back the dagger, ready to spear Tom like a fish. But instead, Tom lunged forward, seizing hold of the middle prong. With a splatter of spray, he felt himself lifted up through the air, still holding on to the redsteel spike.

Let go! the Beast's voice roared in Tom's head. Ignoring it, Tom slashed at the Beast's wrist, his blade thudding hard into Nersepha's scales.

With a screech of pain, Nersepha released Mathilde. The woman dropped like a stone, disappearing among the waves with hardly a splash.

Tom threw himself clear, diving for the water where Mathilde had gone under. Surging deep beneath the surface, he saw her, tunic billowing as she sank. He sheathed his sword, took her in his arms and kicked out, steering them in the direction of the shore.

As Tom swam up above the waves, he heard Nersepha's call again, more savage than ever. He glanced back and felt a jolt at the sight of the Beast racing towards him, mouth gaping wide. She had snapped the shaft of the arrow buried in her shoulder. Her tail writhed like a snake's, driving her through the water with terrifying speed.

Got to swim faster!

Tom powered on, using the magic of the Golden Armour. Up ahead, a string of rocks rose up from the coastline, and Tom headed for them. Figures were hopping across the rocks towards him – conscript sailors, their eyes wide with alarm. The closest was another boy with red hair. "I'm coming, Mother!" he cried.

"She's all right," gasped Tom, as he reached the string of rocks. The boy knelt down and grabbed Mathilde under her arms, heaving her up on to dry land.

Tom was just about to haul himself out of the water too, when he felt something cold and clammy grip his foot. Then he was tugged violently backwards. For an instant the ocean closed over him, filling his ears with a roar and blurring his vision. Then he felt himself lifted upside down from the water, his clothes dripping as he dangled in Nersepha's deadly grip. She lifted him higher until

he was hanging above her head. Her mouth gaped open like a dank cavern, as she threw back her head to swallow him whole.

Not this time, Nersepha! Drawing his sword, Tom swiped and slashed at the Beast's wrist. He felt the blade bite deep, and her grip weaken. Tom fell headfirst and tumbled down into the waves.

Beneath the water, Tom kicked out, swimming towards the middle of the bay. *You won't escape me!* Nersepha's voice hissed in his head. But Tom just swam harder. Up ahead he saw shadowy hulls hanging in the water. He kicked his way behind the closest, where the Beast wouldn't be able to see him.

Tom surfaced and wiped seawater from his eyes. At once, he saw that Ria's mighty armada was setting sail. The vessels moved off, slowly at first, cutting through the water and leaving white wakes behind them as their sails spread taut in the wind.

Tom began to swim, darting in and out of the slipstreams of the vessels, dodging around anchor chains as they were hoisted, and behind ships whenever he could. *Maybe I can lose Nersepha among this fleet...*

At the same time, his heart felt heavy with dread. The first vessels were already out of the bay, heading towards Avantia...

Even if I can escape the Beast, I still need to stop the invasion!

Then Tom saw an anchor bigger than all the others, shimmering red as it swayed, dripping, just above the waves. It was Ria's anchor, and sure enough her flagship was drifting overhead.

If I can just get back on to that ship...

Before he could do a thing, Tom felt a surge of water from behind. Turning, he saw Nersepha's body skimming through the waves, her eyes blazing with fury. *Swwwssh!* Her dagger-hand came down, lunging straight at his face.

FOR MAKAI

Just in time, Tom dodged.

THUMP! The Beast's dagger-hand struck the hull of a ship behind Tom, rocking it in the water. Nersepha howled and tried to drag her hand free, but it was lodged deep in the timbered hull.

Quickly, Tom struck out for the anchor, swimming as fast as he could. But Nersepha soon got her blades free and came after him, with powerful strokes of her tail. With a final burst of speed, Tom launched himself out of the water, his fingertips closing over the cold redsteel of the anchor. He felt himself lurching upwards as the anchor chain was hoisted higher. "Come and get me, Nersepha!" he yelled.

With a screech of rage, the Beast lunged again, driving her dagger-hand straight at Tom. But Tom swung round on the anchor, darting behind the chain. The middle prong of the dagger lodged in one of the links, just missing Tom's face.

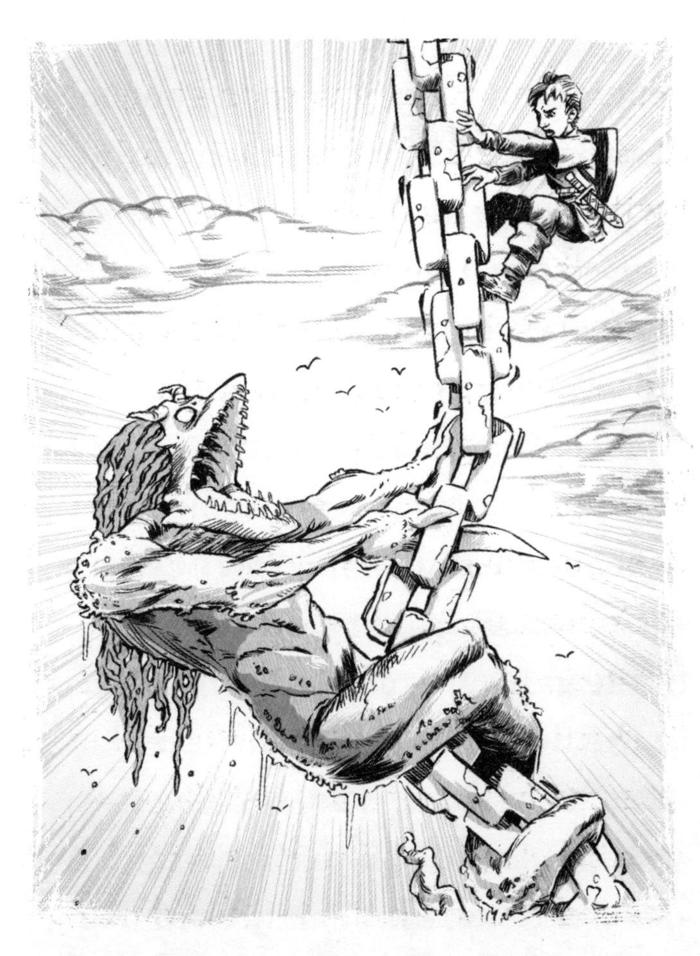

Tom felt the redsteel judder with a sudden strain, and Nersepha screeched again as she was hauled upwards too, along with the anchor. The mermaid Beast writhed, throwing off seawater as she struggled to get her dagger-hand free from the chain. But it was firmly lodged in place.

I will pick your bones clean! Nersepha's voice roared in Tom's head. But Tom could see she was helpless.

Above, he saw that a row of pirate faces had appeared along the edge of the galleon, staring down in shock at the Beast caught on the end of the anchor chain. The whole vessel was listing with the extra weight. A moment later, the chain jerked to a halt, and Tom and Nersepha swayed in midair. *Ria's not going to haul this Beast up on to her deck!*

As Nersepha kept struggling, Tom began to climb the anchor chain, pulling himself towards the ship. There'd be time to face the Beast later. *Got to get to Ria...*

Arms burning from the effort, he vaulted over the gunwale and landed in a crouch on the deck. He drew his sword and unslung his shield, ready for the fight.

"Fire!" yelled someone.

Turning, Tom found himself staring straight into the barrel of a huge cannon set up on the deck. Ria stood beside it, glaring furiously at him.

BOOM!

Tom dived to one side, but not

quite fast enough. The cannonball caught the edge of his shield, and the force spun him round. He skidded into the gunwale with a thump, and collapsed in a heap on the deck. His head spun and his ears rang. He had let go of his sword, he realised, dimly hearing it skittering away across the deck.

The deck shook as pirates charged in from all sides, brandishing their cutlasses.

"No!" screamed Ria. "He's mine!"

The pirates came stumbling to a halt as Ria pushed her way through them, her eyes gleaming with triumph. Her cat-o'-nine-tails crackled in one hand. "Papa always said you were lucky. Let's see how you fight without a weapon."

Tom staggered to his feet, crouching down behind his shield.

Maybe if I can get one of her crew's cutlasses, somehow...

Then Tom heard a wooden creaking sound from overhead. Glancing past the crowd of pirates, he spotted Mathilde's skinny, red-haired son heaving on a rope. Tom's eyes ran up the length of it, and he saw the wooden boom it was attached to swing down low, straight towards Ria's head...

Tom ducked. Ria raised her arms.

CRACK! The boom struck, smacking her on to the deck.

"For Makai!" roared Mathilde's son, as the boom swung free. The other sailors took up the cry, and soon they were all chanting it. "For Makai! For Makai!"

Furious, the pirates turned on the

conscripts. In moments the deck was in chaos as the conscripts snatched up weapons and attacked their captors. The air filled with the clash of metal and the angry shouts of the fighters.

"You..." growled Ria. The pirate captain rose to her feet. She flexed her fingers, and Tom saw bruises blossoming on her forearms. But it looked as though the pain had only enraged her more. "Time to die!"

Ria charged, swinging her flail wildly. Tom rolled across the desk and snatched up his fallen sword. Ria swung again, and Tom had to veer away, leaping up on the gunwale to avoid the electrical sting. He swayed, barely keeping his balance. Ria lashed out once more with her cat-o'-nine-tails. But this time Tom was ready. He met the blow full on with his sword. With a buzz and a crackle, he felt the strands come free, severed by his blade.

As Ria stared at the stump of her flail, Tom launched himself off the gunwale, throwing himself into a somersault in midair and landing on the deck.

Ria tossed the flail aside and picked up a fallen cutlass, curved and deadly. She grunted and swiped skilfully with the blade. Tom danced back, then lunged in himself. He snatched hold of Ria's wrist, keeping his enemy's blade away from him. Then he heaved with all his might, pulling Ria's whole body over his shoulder and thumping her down on to the deck.

Ria lay on her back, groaning. Tom kicked the cutlass from her hand, sending it sliding across the deck.

"This ends now," Tom panted, as he levelled his blade at Ria's throat. "It's over."

The pirate glowered up at him, her face twisted with hatred.

Then, unexpectedly, a horrible smile spread across her features.

"Oh yes, Tom," she said. "It is indeed over...for you."

A shadow fell across the deck, and

Tom felt a prickling cold creep over his skin. He turned round slowly. Towering above them was a huge dark figure, hauling herself over the gunwale. Nersepha's green hair shook with fury, and her eyes latched

on to Tom. She snorted, like a shark scenting blood.

She must have got free of the chain... thought Tom.

But before he could face the Beast, something connected hard with the back of his legs, and he lost his balance. Sprawling on the deck, he saw Ria grinning. *She kicked my feet away from under me!*

"Farewell, Tom," said the pirate, as Nersepha raised her giant, three-pronged dagger, ready to plunge it into Tom's heart...

MUTINY

Tom had no time to think.

Summoning the strength of the golden breastplate, he drew his arm back and hurled his sword. It spun through the air, glinting, straight at Nersepha's wrist. *THUNK!* The blade bit deep, slicing clean through flesh and bone.

Nersepha let out a searing howl.

Her bladed hand fell, severed from her arm. With a soft thump, the three-pronged dagger buried itself in the deck beside Tom.

The Beast shuddered for a moment, as though a strange chill was passing through her. Then – *CRASH!* – her whole body exploded. Tom ducked down behind his shield as Nersepha dissolved into a wave of seawater. He heard it raining down on the deck.

Tom shook the water from his shield and stared in astonishment at the pool of water which had been the Beast.

Has she really gone?

"Nooo!" screeched Ria.

Tom whirled round, just in time to

see her pick up the fallen cutlass once more. All around her on the deck, the fighting still raged between pirates and conscripts, most of them dripping with seawater from the defeated Beast.

"You fool," snarled Ria. "With or without Nersepha, we'll still lay waste to Avantia. I'll crush this little mutiny, then I'll— "

BOOM!

Just beyond the flagship, Tom saw a vessel go up in a sudden surge of purple flames. It dropped from the sky, plunging towards the waves. Ria saw it too, and her jaw fell open.

Tom's heart leaped. *Elenna's plan – it's working!*

"I wouldn't be too sure of that," he told Ria. "Our mutiny might not be quite so little after all."

In the distance, Tom saw another ship explode into purple flame, then another, and another...

"Makai scum!" spat Ria. "How dare they defy me?"

"It's simple," said Tom. "If you rule with fear, you'll never earn true loyalty."

Within moments the whole sky was stained purple, and the heat of the fires washed across the deck of Ria's flagship. Vessels were dropping like flies, and even the fleet on the sea below was half ablaze. Peering closer, Tom saw sailors jumping ship, diving into the water or sliding down ropes to their freedom. On the beach, he could see the tiny figure of Elenna shouting to sailors, organising lifeboats which were heading out into the bay to rescue sailors and pirates alike.

"Tom!" yelled someone nearby. Turning, Tom recognised the red-haired boy who was one of Mathilde's sons. He was sweaty and panting, and held an axe. "I've lit the gunpowder barrels!" he shouted. "The ship's going to blow!"

"What did he say?" barked Ria.

BOOM!

The whole deck shook. Tom saw flames rear up from the prow of

the flagship, chunks of wood and rope flying up into the sky. Sailors and pirates scattered, scrambling away from the fire. Some dived off the gunwales, or swung away on lanyard ropes.

Tom felt the deck begin to pitch as the flagship sank lower in the sky.

"Give it up, Ria," he called, clinging on to the gunwale. "Your invasion is finished."

Ria glared at him, fuming. "You think you're a hero," she jeered. "But really you're just too weak to take what you want! True power belongs to those who grab it with both hands."

"We'll let the people of Makai be the judges of that," said Tom. "This is their island, so they'll decide what you deserve."

Just then, someone behind Tom shouted: "Look out!"

Glancing over his shoulder, Tom

saw a massive galleon looming over them, raining ash as it burned in a fierce purple inferno. It was plunging down towards the flagship, sails flapping as they were engulfed by fire.

It's going to crash into us!

Something hit Tom like a charging bull, sending him sprawling over the deck. Ria was on top of him, crushing him with her weight. Tom writhed, but he couldn't shake her off.

"If I'm going to die," Ria whispered in Tom's ear, "you're dying with me!"

1

THE ISLE OF THE FREE

Tom could feel the heat of the flames, scorching hot as the galleon surged towards them on a collision course. But Ria still hung on, locking him in place.

I've got to get free!

Tom drew deep, summoning the last dregs of magical strength from the golden breastplate. A moment later he felt the power course through his arms and legs, and he shoved hard. Ria went tumbling across the deck, and Tom staggered to his feet. Panting, he held out his hand.

"Over here!" he yelled. "There's still time to jump ship."

Ria stared back at Tom, her scowl lit up purple in the flames, making it look even more savage. Slowly, she shook her head. Then she turned to gaze up at the galleon as it came crashing down towards her.

"Please—" began Tom. But it was too late. A moment before the galleon struck, he grabbed hold of the gunwale and launched himself over the side.

CRRRRASH!

Purple flames billowed all around, barrels and timber flying through the air in all directions. Tom felt the fire scorching his back...

Then he was plummeting through the sky, with the waves rushing towards him.

Tom slung his shield and reached out his arms, turning the fall into a dive. He cut through the water and plunged deep. Then he kicked out, powering back upwards.

Surfacing, Tom spat out seawater and rubbed at his eyes. At once he saw Ria's flagship falling out of the sky, trailing flames like a comet. It struck the water with a hiss and a sizzle of smoke. Then it was gone, leaving only a few bits of flotsam and jetsam bobbing behind it.

In spite of everything, Tom felt a pang in his heart. *She didn't need to die...I could have saved her. If only things had been different. If only she hadn't been the daughter of Sanpao and Kensa...*

Tom looked away. Everywhere, Ria's fleet was in ruins. There were no more ships in the sky. All of them had gone crashing down among the waves. Even the fires were beginning to die out.

It's really over. The invasion of Avantia has been prevented.

Then a familiar voice carried over the waves to him.

"Hey, Master of the Beasts!"

Tom grinned at the sight of Elenna kneeling in the prow of a rowing boat manned by conscripts. She leaned forward and reached out to him. "Need a hand?"

Soon afterwards, Tom stood on a makeshift platform raised up on barrels on the beach. A cool breeze ruffled his hair and dried his sodden tunic. Islanders gathered all around him, filling the sand and stretching back as far as he could see. There were familiar faces among them. Mathilde, together with her three sons, and Isaac and Ezra, and even some workers he recognised from the redsteel mines where he'd defeated Menox. The defeated pirates huddled by the cliff, watched over by stern-faced guards.

"Three cheers for Tom!" cried Mathilde. "Our saviour!"

Tom held up a hand as the cheers died down. "I'm truly grateful," he said. "But it's not me who saved you. It was all of you, working together. You saved yourselves! I could never have defeated Ria and her pirates without your help."

Another ragged cheer rose up from the conscripts, and Mathilde stepped up to shake Tom by the hand. "Nevertheless," said Mathilde, when the crowd finally fell silent, "you showed us the way, Tom. We will never again allow pirates to rule our island with their tyranny. From now on, we shall be Makai no more. We shall be the Isle of the Free!"

Another great cheer followed Mathilde's announcement.

Tom saw Daltec and Elenna weaving through the crowd to join him. Elenna had a sack slung over her shoulder. "These are the tokens we collected from the Beasts," she said, setting the sack down on the platform. "And here's the very last one – the dagger of Nersepha." She drew the triple redsteel blade from

her belt and put it into the sack. "Mathilde's sons found it washed up on the beach."

"They really ought to be

destroyed," said Daltec.

"Don't worry," Tom told him. "I've got a plan for them. I'll make sure they can never be found again."

Taking the sack, Tom hopped down from the platform and made his way to the edge of the beach, where the waves lapped gently at the sand. He kept going, wading out into the water, until it was right up to his waist. Behind him, he could sense Elenna, Daltec and the islanders all watching him silently.

"Are you there, Sepron?" Tom said softly, touching the magical red jewel in his belt.

The sea was still. Then suddenly, a massive green head reared up from the waves, dripping seawater. A murmur ran among the islanders watching from the beach.

"Don't be afraid!" Tom called back to them. "Sepron is a Good

Beast. I summoned him here myself, right after the battle with Nersepha. He's come all the way from Avantia." He turned back to Sepron, offering up the sack. "Take these, old friend. Swim with them to the bottom of the deepest ocean, and leave them far apart, where no one can ever lay hands on them again."

Sepron bowed his head, gently taking the sack in his massive jaws. Then in one smooth motion he was gone, disappearing beneath the waves, with no trace but a gentle wake as he swam out to sea.

"You've saved another kingdom, Tom," said Elenna, as Tom waded back to the shore. "Don't you think it's time we had a rest?"

Tom smiled, but shook his head. "Perhaps for a little while," he said. "I can't wait to get back to Avantia... But I'll never stop fighting Evil – not while there's blood in my veins!"

THE END

CONGRATULATIONS, YOU HAVE COMPLETED THIS QUEST!

At the end of each chapter you were awarded a special gold coin. The QUEST in this book was worth an amazing 8 coins.

Look at the Beast Quest totem picture inside the back cover of this book to see how far you've come in your journey to become

MASTER OF THE BEASTS.

The more books you read, the more coins you will collect!

Do you want your own Beast Quest Totem?

1. Cut out and collect the coin below
2. Go to the Beast Quest website
3. Download and print out your totem
4. Add your coin to the totem

www.beastquest.co.uk/totem

8

Don't miss the first exciting Beast Quest book in this series, MENOX THE SABRE-TOOTHED TERROR!

Read on for a sneak peek...

CELEBRATIONS CUT SHORT

Tom and Elenna pressed through the throng of brightly dressed partygoers crowding the palace courtyard. They passed jugglers, fortune-tellers, jesters and countless traders

calling out from behind market stalls piled high with delicious food or handmade wares. The cheerful melody of pipes and bells filled the square, and everywhere Tom looked he could see the smiling faces of

townsfolk celebrating the safe return of the royal family to the palace.

At the palace doors, a pair of guards waved Tom and Elenna inside. King Hugo and Queen Aroha sat in state in the throne room, their jewelled crowns glittering in the morning sun that slanted through the open windows. Aroha gently rocked Prince Thomas's wicker cradle on a wooden stand at her side. Behind the royal family, Daltec the wizard stood with his mentor, Aduro, both wearing matching dark blue robes covered in stars and moons.

"We've brought gifts for baby Thomas," Elenna said.

"How kind of you!" Queen Aroha said.

Tom and Elenna peered into the cradle. Baby Thomas stared up at them with round blue eyes, his pudgy fists pumping as if he were fighting an imaginary opponent.

"Here you go, Tommy, this is for you," Elenna said, holding a driftwood carving of a wolf towards the child. The baby gurgled and made a jab for the toy, almost knocking it from her hand.

"He's getting strong!" Elenna said, placing the gift beside the baby. Tom lifted the present he'd brought – a soft black cushion stitched in the shape of a stallion. His aunt had made it for him when he was a baby, and he remembered playing with its soft tassels and shiny button eyes. *I hope he likes it!* As Tom leaned over the cot to set his cushion next to Elenna's wolf, baby Thomas let out a squeak and swung his tiny fist, bopping Tom right on the nose.

"Ow!" Tom reeled back in surprise, his eyes watering from the blow.

"Ha!" Hugo said, smiling proudly. Suddenly angry shouting rose above the music and laughter drifting through the windows.

"This way, you scoundrel!" Booted feet stomped along the passageway outside, quickly followed by a heavy rap on the door.

"Come in!" Hugo called, but even before the words were out the chamber door burst open and Admiral Ryker strode through, red-faced and sweating, his chin lifted high as he saluted the king.

"I bring important news!" Ryker cried. Two uniformed officers dragged a sun-browned man wearing tattered rags into the room. The captive's shirt had been torn, showing his ribs; a stubbly beard covered his hollow cheeks. His pale, bloodshot eyes looked wild with fear.

"We apprehended this vagabond after he washed up on the southwestern shore," Ryker said. The

admiral tugged up the prisoner's sleeve, revealing a black pirate skull on the red-brown skin. "He's a spy for the Pirates of Makai."

The captive man flinched. "I'm no pirate!" he croaked. "I was fleeing Makai. The pirates have— "

"Silence!" Ryker shouted.

Tom glanced at the mark on the man's arm and frowned. "King Hugo," he said, "that mark is no tattoo. It's a brand. I think we should hear this man out."

The captive man nodded vigorously, his eyes flicking between Tom and the king.

"Let him speak," Hugo told Ryker.

"But..." Ryker started to protest,

but Hugo silenced him with a stern look. The admiral let the man go.

"Life's always been hard on Makai," said the prisoner, "what with Sanpao's pirates looting and taking their cut of everything – but now his daughter Ria's in charge, it's a thousand times worse. She's got all Sanpao's men working for her and she won't rest until she's taken control of everything and everyone."

Ryker let out a loud sniff. "Ridiculous," he scoffed. "I've seen this Ria. How can a skinny girl take control of a whole kingdom?"

"She managed to sink most of your navy," Elenna muttered.

Ryker opened and shut his mouth,

a fierce blush spreading up his cheeks. "I… "

"Go on," King Hugo told the captive.

"The folk of Makai aren't normally ones to beg," the prisoner said, "but that's what I've come here for. On behalf of all our men, women and children – we need help, and we need it quickly. Sanpao's lass has four Beasts under her control. We don't stand a chance."

Read

MENOX THE SABRE-TOOTHED TERROR

to find out what happens next!

MEET TEAM HERO
FROM ADAM BLADE
THEIR GIFTS MAKE THEM DIFFERENT
NICE HANDS!
FREAK!
BUT WHEN DANGER COMES...
CRACK!
RUMBLE!
SCREEECH!
...A HERO IS BORN
OTHERS WITH GIFTS WILL SEEK THEM OUT...
...AND SHOW THEM THEIR DESTINY.
EVER HEARD OF HERO ACADEMY?
OUT NOW!
TEAM HERO
TEAM HERO
TEAM HERO
TEAM HERO
TEAMHEROBOOKS.CO.UK
DARE TO BE DIFFERENT